The Geeky Brothers...

NAKED IN THE FRONT YARD

MW01681286

A LONG OVERDUE BOOK

John Long

POCKET BOOKS
New York London Toronto Sydney Tokyo Singapore

The cartoons on the cover and in this book have been previously published in syndication and distributed by King Features Syndicate.

This book is a work of fiction. Names, characters, places and incidents are either the product of the author's imagination or are used fictitiously. Any resemblance to actual events or locales or persons, living or dead, is entirely coincidental.

An *Original* publication of POCKET BOOKS

POCKET BOOKS, a division of Simon & Schuster Inc.
1230 Avenue of the Americas, New York, NY 10020

ISBN: 0-671-67972-4

First Pocket Books trade paperback printing December 1990

10 9 8 7 6 5 4 3 2 1

Printed in the U.S.A.

Dedicated to my mom, Iva Long

John Long jams with The Moos Bros. at Dirty Dave's Dive in Monroe, Michigan

© 1989 King Features Syndicate, Inc.
john ong
World rights reserved

NEVER EAT RIBS WHILE
RAKING LEAVES

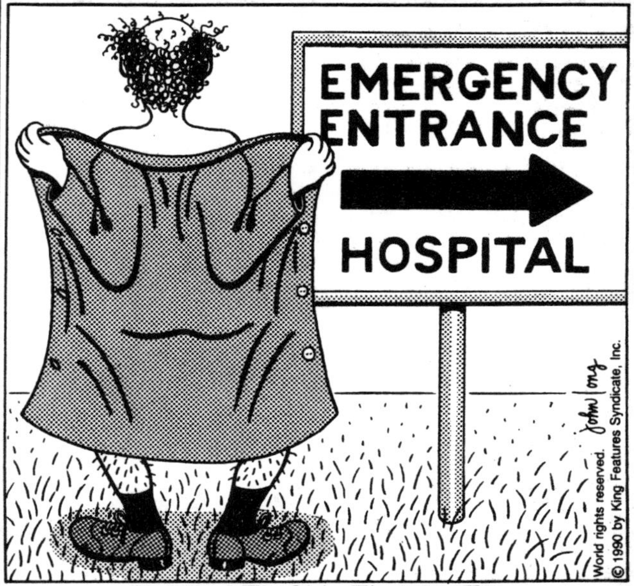
EMERGENCY
ENTRANCE
HOSPITAL
john ong
World rights reserved.
© 1990 by King Features Syndicate, Inc.

EMERGENCY FLASHER

RADIO CITY MOOSIC HALL ... AND STEP ON IT !
THERE'S NO FLIES ON US!
CUD Cola
CUD Cola
I ♥ MOO YORK
© 1990 by King Features Syndicate, Inc. World rights reserved.
john long

THE MOOS BROTHERS IN MOO YORK

john long
World rights reserved.
© 1990 by King Features Syndicate, Inc.

WHEN THE FLEA COLLAR RIDES DOWN

AGE 5
ALBERT
john long
© 1989 King Features Syndicate, Inc. World rights reserved.

A YOUNG ALBERT EINSTEIN WITH A DRAWING HIS TEACHER THOUGHT WAS A TREE

GOODYE
© 1990 by King Features Syndicate, Inc. World rights reserved.

BEWARE OF GEEKS BEARING GIFTS

John Long

FLEM HAS TROUBLE HOLDING HIS LICKER

John Long
© 1990 by King Features Syndicate, Inc. World rights reserved.
THERE'S NOAH BUSINESS LIKE SHOWA BUSINESS... LIKE NOAH BUSINESS I KNOW...

IF NOAH HAD BEEN AN ENTERTAINER

DINNER WAS GOING WELL UNTIL MRS. WATERMELON OFFERED MASHED POTATOES TO MR. AND MRS. POTATO

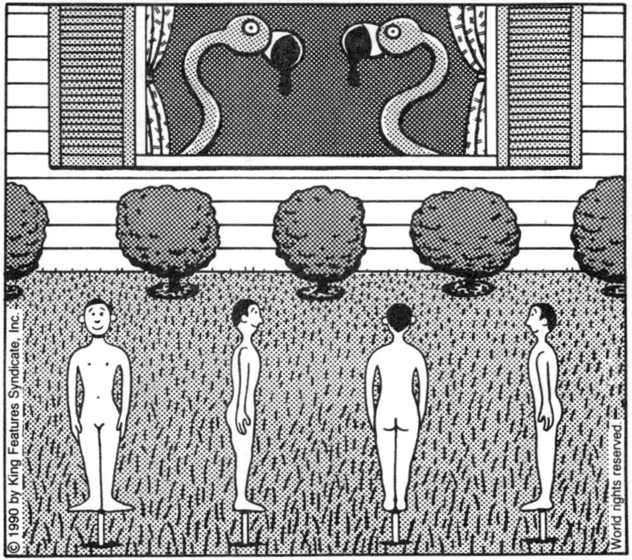
© 1990 by King Features Syndicate, Inc.
World rights reserved.

MR. AND MRS. FLAMINGO ADMIRING THEIR LAWN ORNAMENTS

© 1990 by King Features Syndicate, Inc.
IF THIS WORKS... I'LL BE AS FAT AS GARFIELD
PAINT GRASS GREEN
World rights reserved.
john long

© 1989 King Features Syndicate, Inc. World rights reserved
john long

HOW MR. POTATO HEAD PUTS ON HIS CONTACT LENS

© 1989 King Features Syndicate, Inc.
AGATHA CHRISTIE
STEPHEN KING
john long
World rights reserved
PENCILS OF FAMOUS WRITERS

john long
© 1990 by King Features Syndicate, Inc. World rights reserved.
THE WHEEL WAS DISCOVERED BY ACCIDENT...
RIGHT AFTER THE TINKER TOY ™

© 1990 by King Features Syndicate, Inc. World rights reserved.

THE BADMINTON GOLF BALL...
GOLF COURSES WON'T HAVE TO BE SO LARGE

© 1989 King Features Syndicate, Inc.
World rights reserved

DRACULA'S CHUBBY NEPHEW...
COUNT CALORIES

ROBO
COW
THE HOLSTEIN FAMILY'S FAVORITE MOVIE

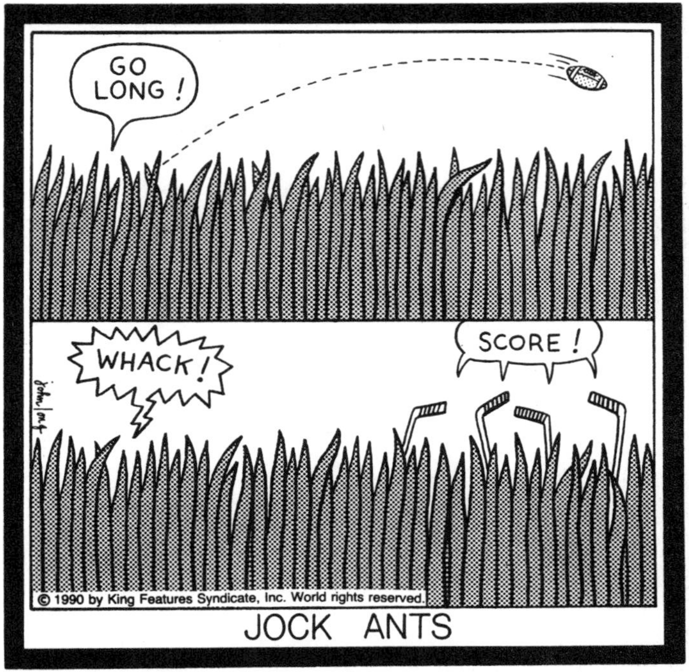
GO LONG!
WHACK!
SCORE!
© 1990 by King Features Syndicate, Inc. World rights reserved.
JOCK ANTS

© 1990 by King Features Syndicate, Inc. World rights reserved.

MR. POTATO HAS AN EXCELLENT POKER FACE

© 1990 by King Features Syndicate, Inc. World rights reserved.

MR. STICKFIGURE SOAKED IN THE TUB TOO LONG

RR
RR
john long

THE WICKED WITCH OF THE WEST COAST

GREEN
john long

LES HAS HEARD SO MUCH ABOUT THE GREENHOUSE EFFECT THAT HE'S DECIDED TO PAINT HIS HOUSE GREEN TO SAVE ON HIS HEATING BILLS

YOU ARE WHAT YOU WEAR
© 1990 by King Features Syndicate, Inc. World rights reserved.
john long

john long
© 1990 by King Features Syndicate, Inc. World rights reserved.
THERE'S ONE BORN EVERY MINUTE

GREAT SUNGLASSES, BARB WHERE'D YOU FIND 'EM ?
IN THE REAR WINDOW OF MY CAR AFTER A REALLY HOT DAY.
john ong
© 1990 by King Features Syndicate, Inc.
World rights reserved.

john ong

A YOUNG PABLO PICASSO WITH HIS DOG...OR CAT...OR...

YOU'RE DISGUSTING !
john long
© 1990 by King Features Syndicate, Inc. World rights reserved.

MR. POTATO . . .CAUGHT
PICKING HIS NOSE

I'M OUT ON THE STREET AND IT SURE IS HARD...
WE ALL AIN'T DRUNKS AND WE ALL AIN'T SLOBS...
I'D LIKE TO HAVE A HOME WITH A NICE BIG YARD...
ALL THAT WE NEED ARE SOME WORTHWHILE JOBS !
STREET NEWS
© 1990 by King Features Syndicate, Inc.
World rights reserved.
john long

BUM RAP

john long

EINSTEIN WARMING UP

john long

THE NEW ALL-YOU-CAN-EAT-
THROUGH-A-COLANDER DIET

INFLATE
-A-
CAT
john long
© 1990 by King Features Syndicate, Inc.
World rights reserved.

THE WORM TURNS

© 1990 by King Features Syndicate, Inc.
World rights reserved.
LIKE WHAT TOTALLY AWESOME GRASS...
GAG ME WITH A BALE OF HAY
john long

A VALLEY COW

TAKE -A- NUMBER
1
john long
ORGANIZED CRIME

HISTORICAL LANDMARK
BIRTHPLACE OF
MICKEY MOUSE
john long

I GUESS HATS ARE OUT.
© 1990 by King Features Syndicate, Inc. World rights reserved.

MR. POTATO THINKS THAT MRS. POTATO'S NEW FACE-LIFT MAY BE A LITTLE TOO HIGH

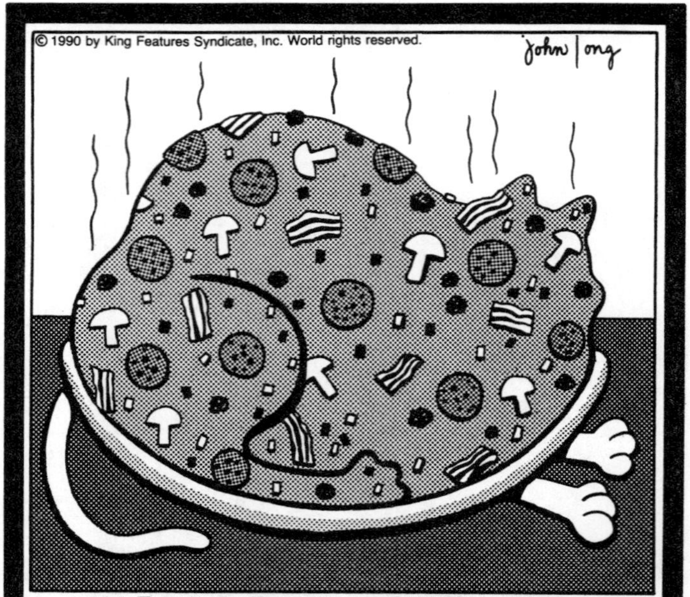
© 1990 by King Features Syndicate, Inc. World rights reserved.

WHILE NO ONE WAS LOOKING . . . THE CAT FOUND A WARM SPOT UNDER THE PIZZA

john long
© 1990 by King Features Syndicate, Inc. World rights reserved.

BIG BOY GETTING READY FOR WORK

I KNOW YOU ARE
BUT WHAT AM I ?
PROPERTY OF THE VATICAN
john long

PEE-WEE HERMAN MEETS THE POPE

© 1989 King Features Syndicate, Inc. World rights reserved
John Long

INSTEAD OF WAKING UP ON THE WRONG SIDE OF THE BED ... FLEM JUST SNEAKS OUT OF A CORNER

HOLY KILOWATTS!
© 1990 by King Features Syndicate, Inc. World rights reserved.
John Long

GOD RECEIVING THE FIRST LIGHT BILL

YOU MUST PICK ONE
RAIN ALL DAY
OR
HOT AS HELL
© 1990 by King Features Syndicate, Inc.
World rights reserved.
john long

PICNICKER'S HELL

john long

LA DAIRYÈRE

LOVE THE ONE YOU'RE WITH
© 1990 by King Features Syndicate, Inc.
World rights reserved.

I THINK I'LL TRY SOCCER
World rights reserved.
© 1990 by King Features Syndicate, Inc.

MR. POTATO HAS A PROBLEM WITH SLAM DUNKS

© 1990 by King Features Syndicate, Inc.
HEY DAD...WOULD YOU HELP ME WITH MY TIE... I CAN ONLY GET IT A PART TIED.
YOU CAN DO IT BY YOURSELF... JUST BE PATIENT AND MAKE BOTH ENDS EQUAL.
john long
World rights reserved.

A YOUNG NELSON MANDELA

© 1990 by King Features Syndicate, Inc.
World rights reserved.
john long

VELCROQUET...IT'S EASY IF YOU STICK TO IT

john|ong
© 1989 King Features Syndicate, Inc. World rights reserved

HEREDITY HAS A CRUEL SENSE OF HUMOR

© 1989 King Features Syndicate, Inc. World rights reserved
john|ong

IF NOAH HAD BEEN FROM THE CITY

© 1990 by King Features Syndicate, Inc.
World rights reserved.

SALVADOR DALI'S CHRISTMAS TREE

ROBIN USING THE SEXY-WORM ATTACK MANEUVER

World rights reserved
© 1989 King Features Syndicate, Inc.

MR. POTATO JUST DISCOVERED THAT HE WAS SERVED POTATO PANCAKES BY MISTAKE

WHY ?
HOW COME ?
WHAT FOR ?
© 1989 King Features Syndicate, Inc.
World rights reserved

MARK DECIDED TO GROW A BEARD UNLIKE ANYONE ELSE'S...IT WAS SO UNUSUAL THAT PEOPLE BEGAN TO QUESTION MARK

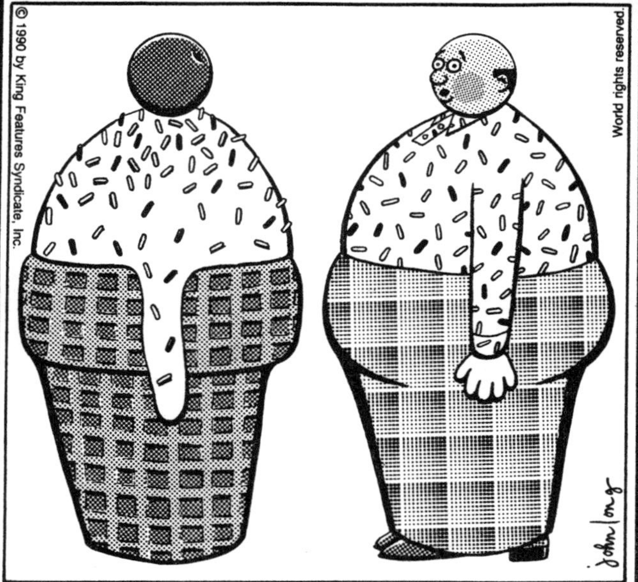
© 1990 by King Features Syndicate, Inc.
World rights reserved.
john long

YOU ARE WHAT YOU EAT

© 1990 by King Features Syndicate, Inc.
World rights reserved.
john long
Chewie
Darth
C3PO

THE EMPIRE STRIKES BACK

DO NOT FEED
World rights reserved.
john ong
© 1990 by King Features Syndicate, Inc.
THE VELCRO TEST AREA

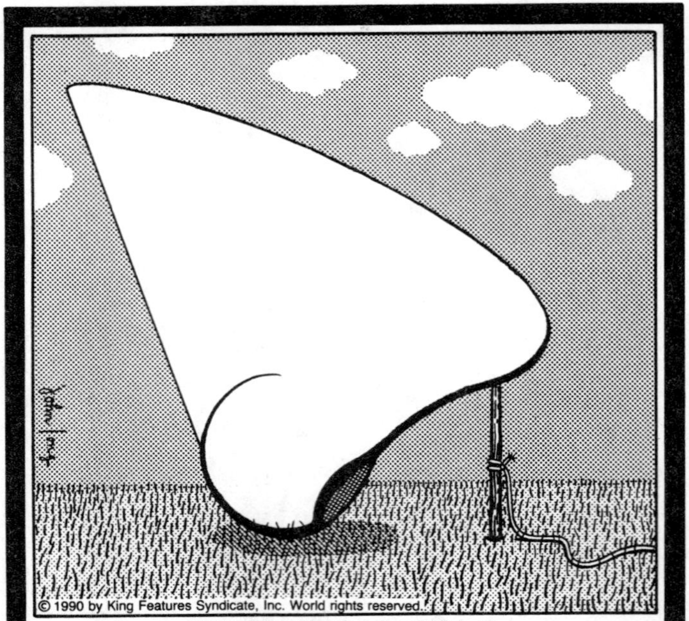
john ong
© 1990 by King Features Syndicate, Inc. World rights reserved.
CATCHING A COLD

WHAT'S THE HOUSE WINE?
WE WANT A RAISE... WE WANT A RAISE.
CAFE WOWDEWOW
john long

SAFE!
john long

MR. POTATO HAS LEARNED HIS LESSON ABOUT SLIDING IN... FACE FIRST

LET SUMMER BEGIN!
THE MOOS BROS.
LET THE DIET BEGIN... HE LOOKS LIKE TEN POUNDS OF MEATLOAF IN A FIVE-POUND PAN.

© 1989 King Features Syndicate, Inc.
World rights reserved.

CAT USING THE FAKE-LAWN-MOWER MANEUVER

YOU'RE SO UGLY... YOU MUST'VE BEEN HIT BY THE UGLY STICK!
john long
© 1990 by King Features Syndicate, Inc. World rights reserved.

STICKFIGURES CAN BE CRUEL

© 1990 by King Features Syndicate, Inc.
World rights reserved.
TOP
NO PASSING ZONE
ONE WA
R R
CAUTION SPEED BUMP
john long

LES IS A REAL ROADS SCHOLAR

HOW DO YOU LIKE ME SO FAR ?
© 1990 by King Features Syndicate, Inc. World rights reserved.

© 1990 by King Features Syndicate, Inc. World rights reserved.
ADD WATER
RUB

DID THE VERY FIRST BAR OF SOAP COME WITH INSTRUCTIONS ?

E=MC2
E=EATING
M=MORE
C=CALORIES
john long

EINSTEIN FINALLY FIGURES OUT WHY HE'S BEEN GAINING WEIGHT

john long

A YOUNG GEORGE ARMSTRONG CUSTER TEASING THE GIRLS IN HIS CLASS

Z Z Z Z
Z Z Z
World rights reserved. John Long © 1990 by King Features Syndicate, Inc.
ELEFENCE

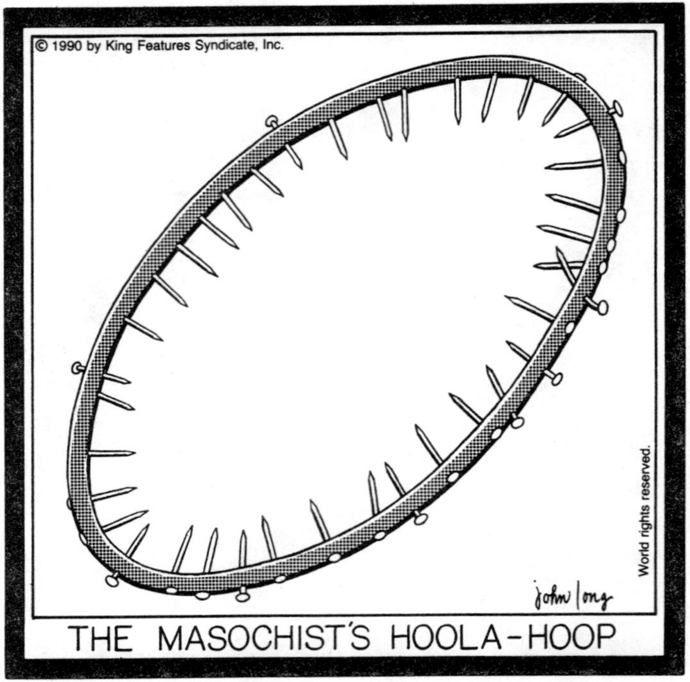
© 1990 by King Features Syndicate, Inc.
World rights reserved.
John Long
THE MASOCHIST'S HOOLA-HOOP

TOMORROW AT THE PICNIC YOU'LL BE SQUASHED BY A TALL DARK STRANGER
CLAIRVOYANT
© 1990 by King Features Syndicate, Inc. World rights reserved.

WINSTON'S PUPPY PHILOSOPHY:
GOOD FOOD... GOOD DOG
BAD FOOD... BAD DOG!
I'LL START BY CHEWING HOLES IN THE GARDEN HOSE
WINSTON
WINSTON
© 1990 by King Features Syndicate, Inc. World rights reserved.

HELLTH FOOD
HAVE A BAD DAY
BEAN SPROUT SALAD 4.95
TOFU SANDWICH 2.95
WHEAT GERM OMELETE 3.25
BEE POLLEN COOKIES .50
CARROT JUICE 2.00
*ALL MEALS COME WITH A SIDE OF NUCLEAR WASTE
© 1990 by King Features Syndicate, Inc. World rights reserved.

© 1990 by King Features Syndicate, Inc. World rights reserved.
THE KU KLUTZ KLAN

© 1989 King Features Syndicate, Inc. World rights reserved
FRED
BARNEY

PREHISTORIC BOWLING BALLS

© 1989 King Features Syndicate, Inc.
World rights reserved

SUMOO WRESTLING

john long
FLEM WOKE UP IN A CLOSET WITH A BAD HANGOVER

I THINK... THEREFORE I YAM
john long
TRANSCENDENTAL VEGETATION

MR. R. GYLE'S STRANGE BIRTHMARK COVERS 90% OF HIS BODY... ONLY HIS ANKLES AND FEET ARE NORMAL

ARCHAEOLOGISTS UNEARTHING THE LARGEST CHOCOLATE CHIP EVER FOUND

DEAR, HAVE YOU SEEN MY BOWLING BALL ?
© 1990 by King Features Syndicate, Inc. World rights reserved.
john long

LOOKS LIKE ANOTHER STORY FOR "UNSOLVED MYSTERIES"

LESLIE
FRED
STAN
2
13
7
4
john long

"DUE TO DEER-HUNTING SEASON... BLITZEN, COMET AND PRANCER WILL BE REPLACED BY LESLIE, FRED AND STAN"

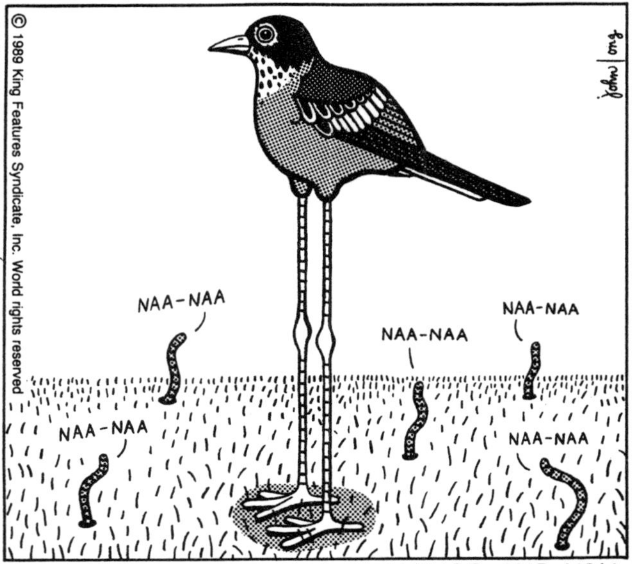
NAA-NAA
NAA-NAA
NAA-NAA
NAA-NAA
NAA-NAA
john ong

CROSS A ROBIN WITH A FLAMINGO AND YOU GET A BIRD THAT WILL STARVE TO DEATH

5 O'CLOCK
SHADOW
john ong

LES HAS A REAL PROBLEM WITH 5 O'CLOCK SHADOW

© 1990 by King Features Syndicate, Inc. World rights reserved.
TOO COOL TO DROOL
The FURBALLS FROM HELL WORLD TOUR
john long
WINSTON AND KIK WEARING THEIR FAVORITE SHIRTS

© 1989 King Features Syndicate, Inc.
World rights reserved
john long
MRS. POTATO DISCOVERS THAT YOU CAN'T PUT 10 POUNDS OF POTATOES IN A FIVE-POUND BAG

THIS IS GREAT! BUT NO ONE CAN SEE MY NEW OUTFIT
© 1990 by King Features Syndicate, Inc. World rights reserved.
john long

DEEP POWDER

TIME TO DO YOUR HOMEWORK, DEAR
LET MY PEOPLE GO
PEOPLE
MAGAZINE
CHER
WHO CARES?
ROB LOWE
WHO CARES?
FLEM
john long
© 1989 King Features Syndicate, Inc. World rights reserved

THE GREAT, GREAT, GREAT, GREAT, GREAT, GREAT, GREAT GRANDSON OF MOSES

CUD LITE
TAN DARK
© 1989 King Features Syndicate, Inc.
World rights reserved

ROAST BEEF

john ong
World rights reserved.
© 1990 by King Features Syndicate, Inc.

WHERE BABY LAWN ORNAMENTS COME FROM

THAT'S THE BIGGEST WORM I EVER CAUGHT !
YOU SHOULD HAVE IT MOUNTED AND HANG IT IN YOUR DEN
World rights reserved.
© 1990 by King Features Syndicate, Inc.

ROBINS RETURNING FROM THE HUNT

THE EARLY BIRD
© 1990 by King Features Syndicate, Inc.
World rights reserved.

MR. ROBIN'S DEN

© 1989 King Features Syndicate, Inc. World rights reserved

WHEN MR. POTATO HEAD GETS BAGS UNDER HIS EYES ... HE JUST GETS BIGGER EYES

© 1990 by King Features Syndicate, Inc.
World rights reserved.

A RECENT DISCOVERY...KING KONG'S THONGS

© 1990 by King Features Syndicate, Inc. World rights reserved.

PEOPLE WHO LIVE IN GLASS HOUSES
SHOULDN'T THROW CONES

NO SCREEN CAN KEEP ME OUT!
© 1990 by King Features Syndicate, Inc. World rights reserved.

A MOSQUITO ON STEROIDS

© 1990 by King Features Syndicate, Inc.
World rights reserved.
john long

MR. SNOWMAN STRUGGLING
WITH WATER RETENTION

john long

CHEATAH

john ong

POCKET CHANGE

THAT'S ENOUGH TV YOU GO OUTSIDE AND PLAY !

JUNIOR STICKFIGURE HAS BEEN WATCHING TOO MUCH MISTER ROGERS

© 1990 by King Features Syndicate, Inc. World rights reserved.

MS. POTATO ENJOYS IRONING IN THE RAW

© 1990 by King Features Syndicate, Inc. World rights reserved.

MRS. WATERMELON NOTICES THAT VERTICAL LINES ONLY SLENDERIZE IF YOU'RE ALREADY SLENDER

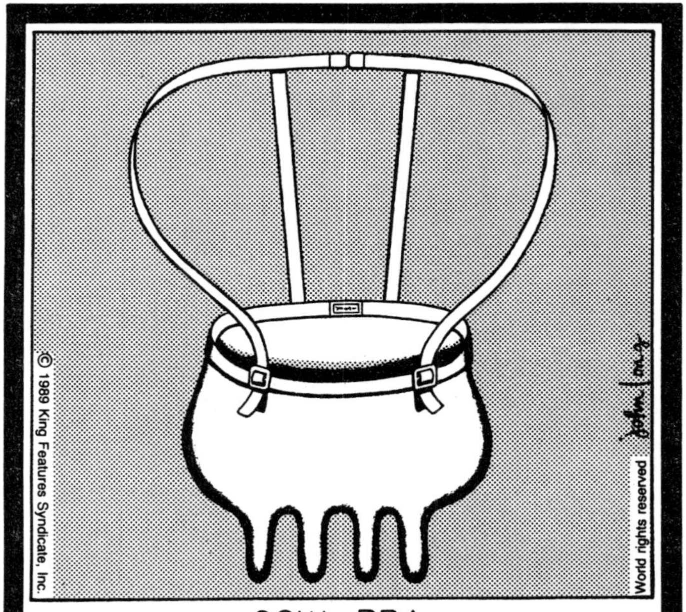
© 1989 King Features Syndicate, Inc.
john long
World rights reserved

COW BRA

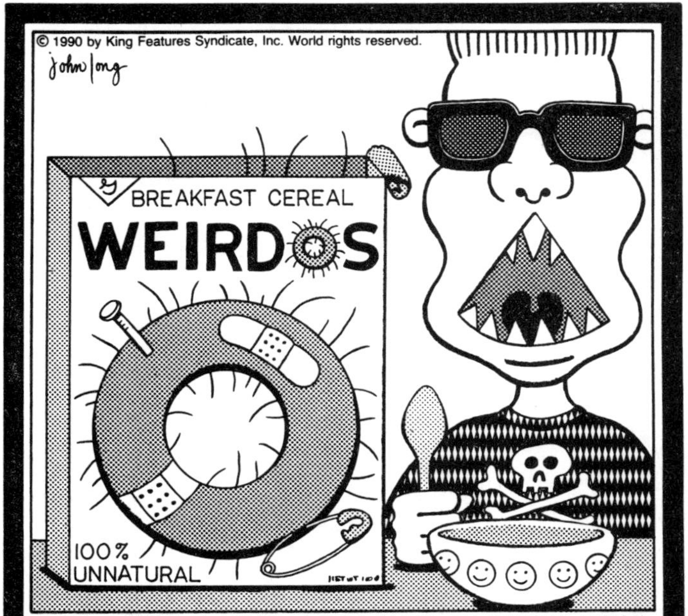
© 1990 by King Features Syndicate, Inc. World rights reserved.
john long
BREAKFAST CEREAL
WEIRDOS
100% UNNATURAL

FOR PEOPLE WHO LIKE HAIR IN THEIR FOOD

© 1990 by King Features Syndicate, Inc. World rights reserved.
WINSTON

FLEA COLLAR ESCAPE TECHNIQUE #1

© 1990 by King Features Syndicate, Inc.
World rights reserved.
E=MC2

EINSTEIN ABOUT TO DISCOVER THE THEORY OF RELATIVITY......AND CHILD SUPPORT

THUNDER-THIGHS
250 CALORIES
FAT
© 1990 by King Features Syndicate, Inc.
World rights reserved.
john long
DONUTS SHOULD COME WITH WARNING LABELS

john long
MEDUSA AS A CHILD

© 1990 by King Features Syndicate, Inc.
World rights reserved.
john long

MR. POTATO'S BEEN DOING LOTS OF SIT-UPS

john long

FAT CHANCE

© 1989 King Features Syndicate, Inc. World rights reserved

EARLY SIGNS OF LEAD POISONING

© 1989 King Features Syndicate, Inc. World rights reserved
john long

ZEUS' NEPHEW, OBESEOUS...
GOD OF CHOCOLATE CAKE

BALLET
PARKING

FLEM CASTS ALL REMAINING SEXUAL HANG-UPS TO THE WIND . . . AND CATCHES A COLD

HOW ARE WE GONNA GET THESE HOME?
YOU'LL SEE...
LIFESAVERS®
WEEEEEEEE
YAHOOOOOOOO
YIPEEEEEEEEE

ANTics

WHAT FOSSILS OF THE FUTURE WILL LOOK LIKE (FAST FOOD)

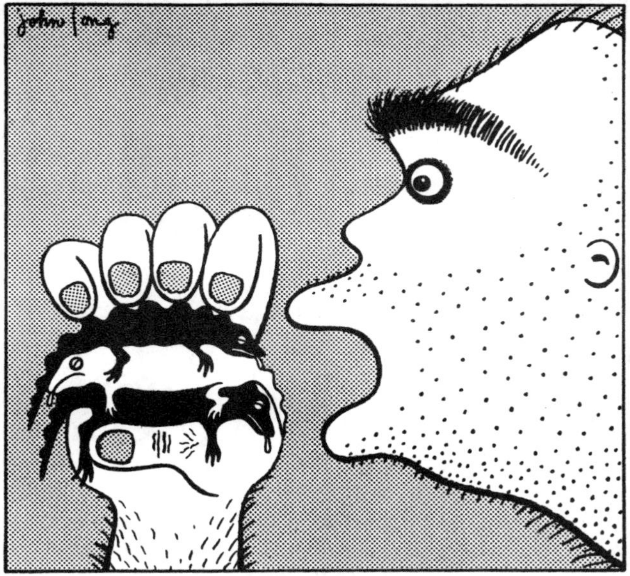

PREHISTORIC OREO

ALL BEEF PATTY
MILK DUD
GROUND CHUCK
john long
© 1990 by King Features Syndicate, Inc. World rights reserved

A NERD HERD

DEAR... I THINK WE'VE HAD ENOUGH SUN
NOT YET... I'M ONLY HALF-BAKED
VEGETABLE 100% OIL
DARK O SKIN
john long
© 1990 by King Features Syndicate, Inc. World rights reserved.

MR. POTATO... BORN TO BAKE

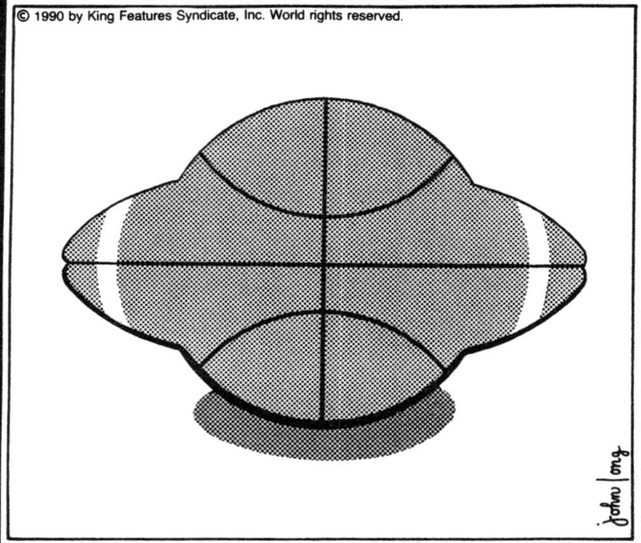
john long

THE NEW COMBINATION BASKETBALL-FOOTBALL MAKES BOTH GAMES MORE INTERESTING

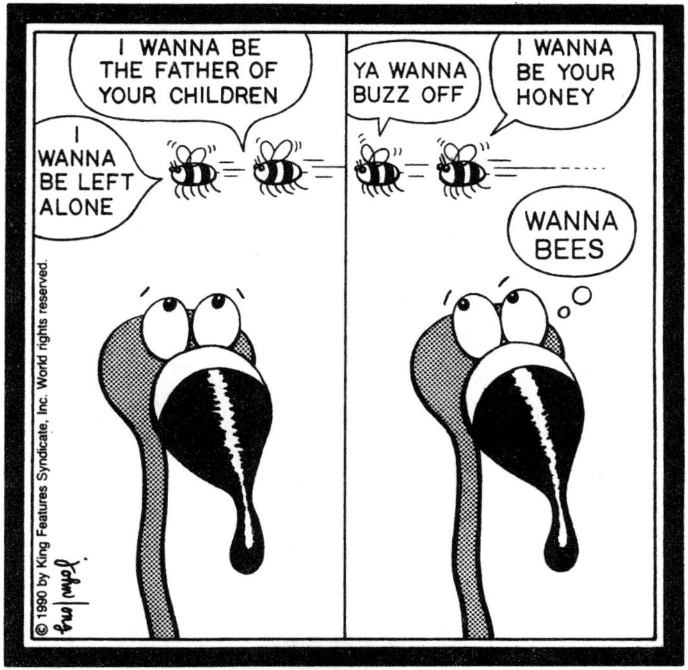
I WANNA BE THE FATHER OF YOUR CHILDREN
I WANNA BE LEFT ALONE
YA WANNA BUZZ OFF
I WANNA BE YOUR HONEY
WANNA BEES
john long

AND IF ELECTED I PROMISE LAND WITHIN ONE WEEK ... TWO WEEKS TOPS

IF NOAH HAD BEEN A POLITICIAN

SO ... WHAT TIME YOU GET OFF WORK ?
john long
World rights reserved.
© 1990 by King Features Syndicate, Inc.

A REAL LONELY ROBIN

World rights reserved.
© 1990 by King Features Syndicate, Inc.
john long

THE GEEKY BROTHERS WITH A FEW EXAMPLES OF THEIR EXTENSIVE ART COLLECTION

'TIS THE SEASON FOR ROAD CONSTRUCTION...
FA-LA-LA-LA-LA-LA-LA-LA-LA
CLOSE THE LEFT LANE...
CLOSE THE RIGHT LANE
FA-LA-LA-LA-LA-LA-LA-LA-LA
CONSTRUCTION NEXT 200 MILES
World rights reserved.
© 1990 by King Features Syndicate, Inc.
john long

SANTA'S SUMMER VACATION

AND THEN SHE SAID ..."YOU HAVE NO IDEA WHAT IT'S LIKE TO BE A FEMALE UNTIL YOU WALK A MILE IN MY SHOES."..

WINSTON'S CONSCIOUSNESS HAS BEEN RAISED BY A 3" HEEL

MR. POTATO'S AT THAT AGE WHEN HE OCCASIONALLY LEAVES HIS FLY OPEN

TIME
© 1990 by King Features Syndicate, Inc. World rights reserved

TIME'S FUN WHEN YOU'RE HAVING FLIES

© 1990 by King Features Syndicate, Inc.
World rights reserved.
HOW WAS YOUR DAY AT SCHOOL, DEAR ?
RELATIVE TO WHAT ? I NEED A POINT OF REFERENCE IN ORDER TO FORMULATE AN EQUATION SUFFICIENT TO ANSWER YOUR QUESTION.
E = ?
GO TO YOUR ROOM !

A YOUNG ALBERT EINSTEIN

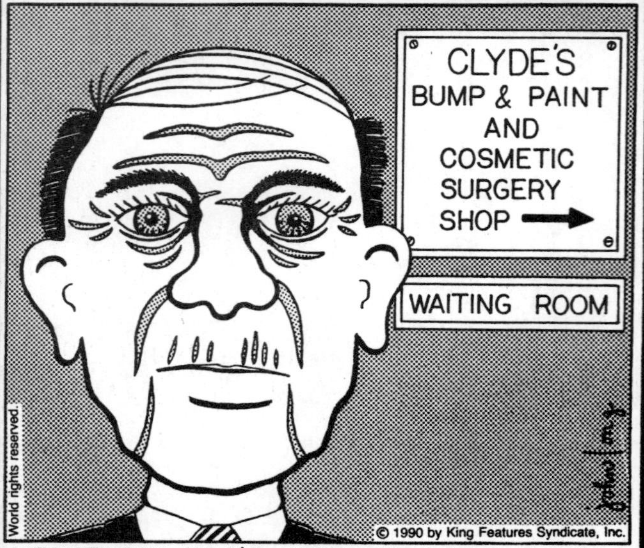
CLYDE'S
BUMP & PAINT
AND
COSMETIC
SURGERY
SHOP
WAITING ROOM
World rights reserved.
© 1990 by King Features Syndicate, Inc.
john long

YESTERDAY BILL'S WRINKLES WERE FILLED IN AND SANDED... TODAY HE GETS PRIMED AND A NEW COAT OF PAINT

DO YOU KNOW HOW MANY CALORIES ARE IN A MALT ?...
YOU CAN'T DRINK FROM A STRAW WITH A BEAK...
AREN'T YOU MISSING "FALCON CREST" ON TV ?...
john long
© 1990 by King Features Syndicate, Inc. World rights reserved.

THE MALT TEASE FALCON

IF YOU WANNA BE HAPPY FOR THE REST OF YOUR LIFE, NEVER MAKE A PRETTY BEE YOUR WIFE... SO FOR MY PERSONAL POINT OF VIEW, GET AN UGLY BEE TO MARRY YOU...
The Wanna Bees
© 1990 by King Features Syndicate, Inc.
World rights reserved.
john long

THE WANNA BEES...ON THEIR STING-LIKE-HELL WORLD TOUR

THE LEAVES ARE SO BAD THIS YEAR THAT IN ORDER TO KEEP UP... FLEM DOES SOME NIGHT RAKING

GRISTLE
© 1989 King Features Syndicate, Inc.
World rights reserved

SUBLIMINAL DEFENSE MECHANISM

MOUSEY
McNUGGETS
© 1990 by King Features Syndicate, Inc.
World rights reserved.

KIK LOVES MOUSEY McNUGGETS

© 1989 King Features Syndicate, Inc.
World rights reserved
john long

MICKEY MOUSSE

© 1989 King Features Syndicate, Inc. World rights reserved
BLOOD'S TURF
CHICO '89
HAVE A YUCKY DAY
NO NUKES
KILLER
RATS

SAFETY TIP...ALWAYS TRAVEL IN PAIRS

© 1989 King Features Syndicate, Inc. World rights reserved
John Long

IT HAPPENS EVERY TIME MRS. POTATO USES TOO MUCH LIPSTICK

© 1990 by King Features Syndicate, Inc.
World rights reserved.
John Long

I WISH HE'D TURN AROUND
LION
© 1990 by King Features Syndicate, Inc. World rights reserved.
EINSTEIN AT THE ZOO

DUE TO NUMEROUS COMPLAINTS CONCERNING THE USE OF THE WORDS BUNS, BUTT, RUMP, REAR, ETC., IN THE COMICS ... FUTURE REFERENCES TO OUR SIT-DOWN PART WILL BE REFERRED TO AS "THIGH TOPS". THANK YOU.
MS. ERY
CARTOON CENSOR
© 1990 by King Features Syndicate, Inc. World rights reserved.

© 1990 by King Features Syndicate, Inc.
World rights reserved.
BURGERS
FRENCH FRIES

MR. POTATO IS UPSET WITH JUNIOR
FOR ORDERING FRENCH FRIES

© 1990 by King Features Syndicate, Inc. World rights reserved.

MRS. STICKFIGURE HAS BECOME VERY DISTANT…
EVER SINCE HER COSMETIC SURGERY

BIG
BOY
Z
Z
Z
Z
Z
Z
Z
BIG
BOY
john | m.g.

BIG BOY'S ROOM

LUCY IN THE SKY WITH DIAMONDS

LAP LAP
LAP
LAP
© 1990 by King Features Syndicate, Inc. World rights reserved.
WINSTON LOVES TO DO LAPS IN THE POOL

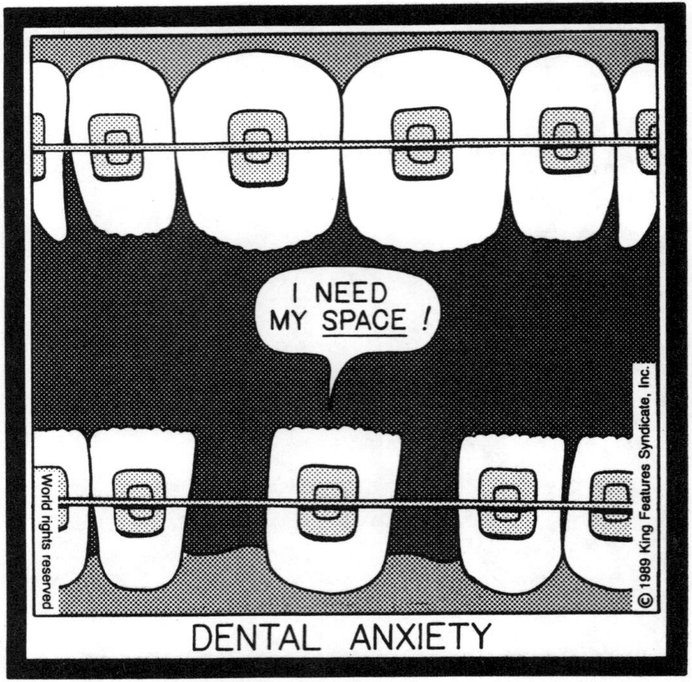
I NEED MY SPACE !
World rights reserved
© 1989 King Features Syndicate, Inc.
DENTAL ANXIETY

JOHN

YOUNG JOHN JAMES AUDUBON AND HIS FIRST BIRD DRAWING

© 1990 by King Features Syndicate, Inc.
World rights reserved.

A COW WITH FAST-FOOD PARANOIA WEARING A BURGER ALARM

© 1990 by King Features Syndicate, Inc. World rights reserved.

FLEM HATES BRAIN STORMS...
IT MESSES UP HIS HAIR

© 1990 by King Features Syndicate, Inc. World rights reserved.

MR. POTATO'S SHOES ARE A
REAL PAIN TO PUT ON

MARTY
© 1989 King Features Syndicate, Inc. World rights reserved

TO BE BORN FUNNY-LOOKING IS BAD ENOUGH, BUT TO ALSO LIVE IN NEW ORLEANS AND BE NAMED MARTY GRAW IS MORE THAN ANYONE SHOULD HAVE TO ENDURE

IT'LL NEVER GET OFF THE GROUND
© 1989 King Features Syndicate, Inc. World rights reserved

IF NOAH HAD BEEN A BRICKLAYER

John Long
© 1990 by King Features Syndicate, Inc. World rights reserved.

THE WORM TURNS

© 1990 by King Features Syndicate, Inc. World rights reserved.
John Long

WHAT ANTS DO DURING THE WINTER

THAT'S A LOT OF CLAMS FOR A DINOSAUR BONE CHAIR
SOLD
john long
© 1990 by King Features Syndicate, Inc. World rights reserved.

DID EARLY MAN GO ANTIQUING ?

HA HA HA
HA HA HA
john long
© 1990 by King Features Syndicate, Inc. World rights reserved.

CROSS A FLAMINGO WITH A TURKEY...
AND YOU'RE TALKING REALLY BAD DRUMSTICKS

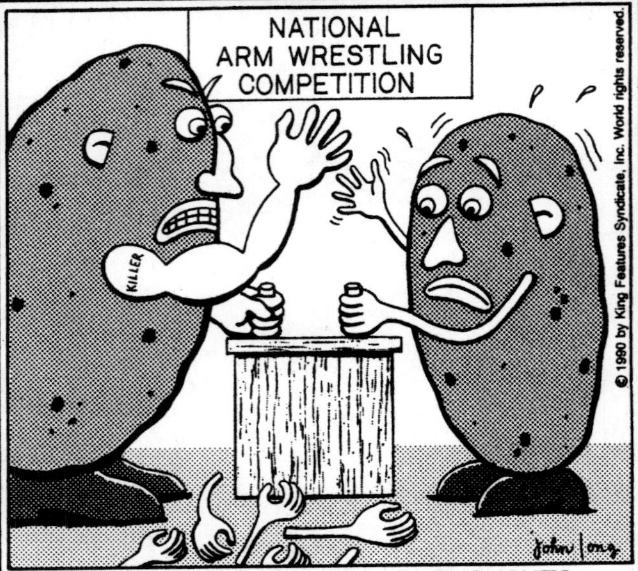
NATIONAL ARM WRESTLING COMPETITION
KILLER
© 1990 by King Features Syndicate, Inc. World rights reserved.

MR. POTATO HAS SECOND THOUGHTS ABOUT CHALLENGING THE CHAMP

© 1990 by King Features Syndicate, Inc. World rights reserved.

CAT USING THE FAKE-BIRDBATH ATTACK MANEUVER

© 1989 King Features Syndicate, Inc. World rights reserved

GUTTER GLASSES...KEEP THE SWEAT OUT OF YOUR EYES

DAMN KINKS
© 1990 by King Features Syndicate, Inc. World rights reserved.

THE NEW ALL-YOU-CAN-SUCK-THROUGH-A-FIFTY-FOOT-GARDEN-HOSE DIET

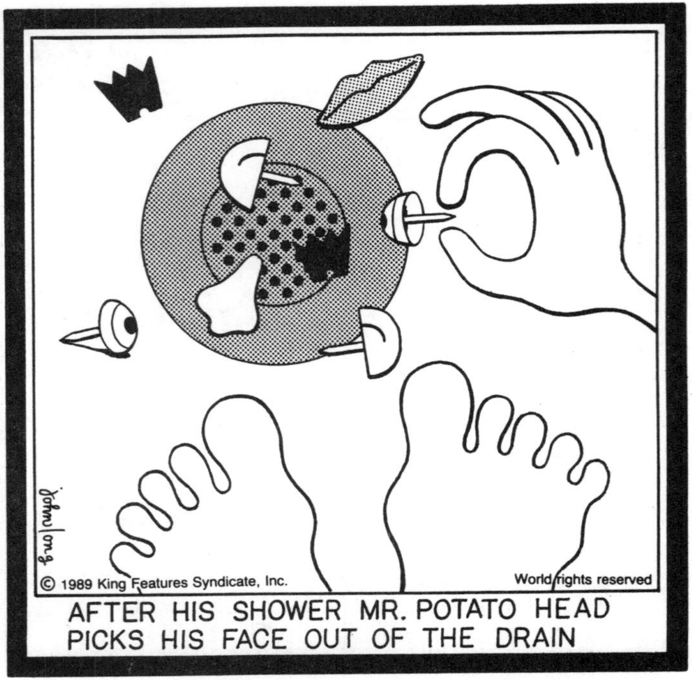
john long
© 1989 King Features Syndicate, Inc.
World rights reserved
AFTER HIS SHOWER MR. POTATO HEAD
PICKS HIS FACE OUT OF THE DRAIN

© 1990 by King Features Syndicate, Inc. World rights reserved.
PICASSO'S
BREAKFAST CEREAL
MOST PEOPLE DON'T UNDER-
STAND IT... BUT THEY KNOW
IT'S GOOD!!!
john long

© 1989 King Features Syndicate, Inc. World rights reserved
john long

MICKEY MOOS

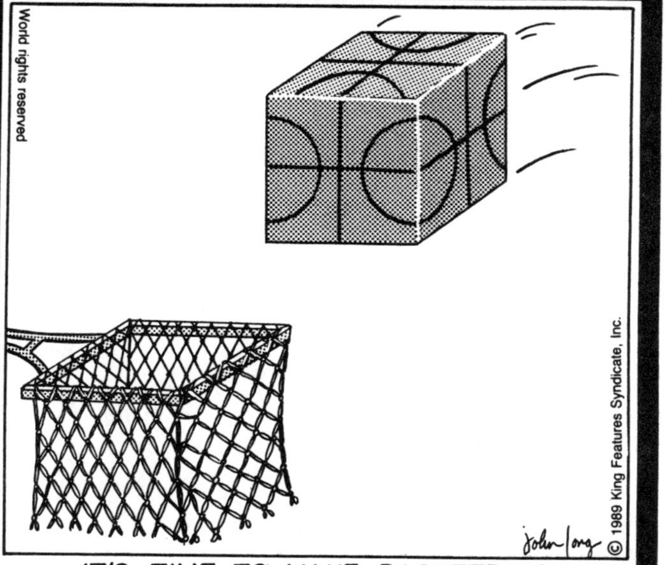

World rights reserved
© 1989 King Features Syndicate, Inc.
john long

IT'S TIME TO MAKE BASKETBALL MORE OF A CHALLENGE

World rights reserved.
© 1990 by King Features Syndicate, Inc.

PRICKLY HEAT

MAYBE I SHOULDA USED COLD WATER
© 1990 by King Features Syndicate, Inc.
World rights reserved.
john long

APPLE THIEVES WILL BE SHOT!
FARMER BROWN

YOUNG ISAAC NEWTON ABOUT TO DISCOVER THE GRAVITY OF THE SITUATION

THIS DONUT HAS BEEN SANITIZED FOR YOUR PROTECTION

john long
© 1990 by King Features Syndicate, Inc. World rights reserved.

THE SMOKE-DETECTOR CAP...FOR THOSE WHO REALLY WANT TO QUIT SMOKING

john long
© 1989 King Features Syndicate, Inc. World rights reserved
CAREFUL... THERE MAY BE MORE
WOW
IT FELL FROM UP THERE !!

A LITTLE SLICE OF HEAVEN

© 1990 by King Features Syndicate, Inc.; World rights reserved.

DURING FLEA SEASON...WINSTON GOES THROUGH DOZENS OF FLEA COLLARS

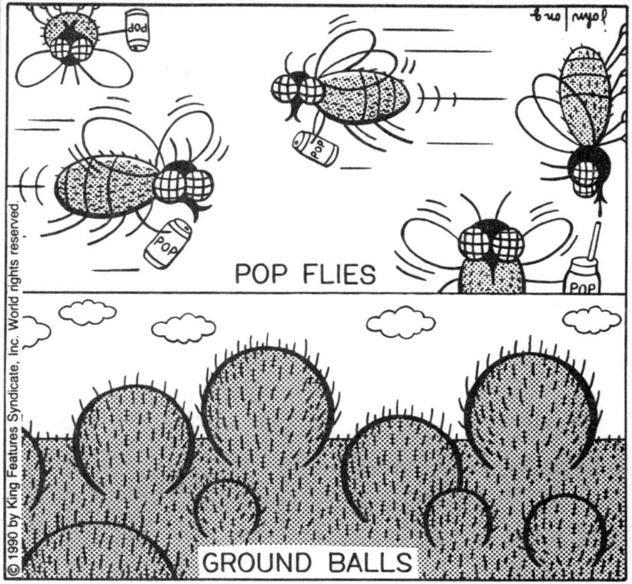
POP
POP FLIES
GROUND BALLS
© 1990 by King Features Syndicate, Inc. World rights reserved.

COMMON BASEBALL TERMS

MOVE... OR YOU'RE SLAW
© 1990 by King Features Syndicate, Inc. World rights reserved.
john long

IT'S DIFFICULT FOR MR. POTATO TO GET ANY SUN WITH MR. CARROT AROUND

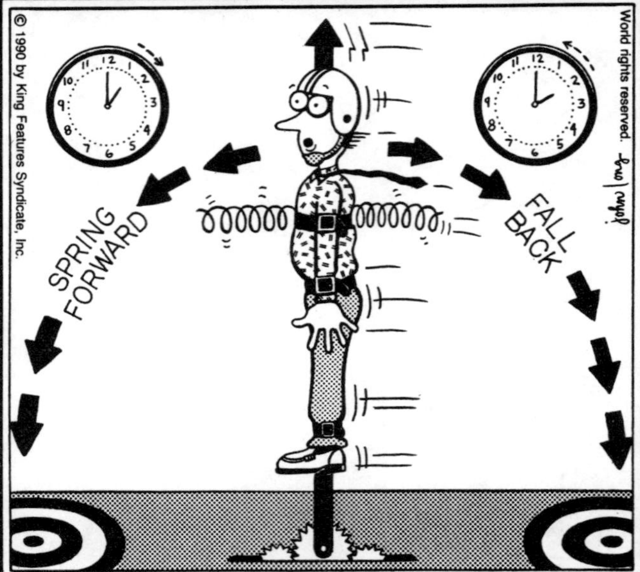
SPRING FORWARD
FALL BACK
© 1990 by King Features Syndicate, Inc.
World rights reserved.
john long

MORTY ALWAYS NEEDS A LITTLE REMINDER TO CHANGE THE TIME ON HIS CLOCKS

World rights reserved
© 1989 King Features Syndicate, Inc.

JOCK LAWN ORNAMENTS

E=MC2
© 1989 King Features Syndicate, Inc. World rights reserved

EINSTEIN ABOUT TO DISCOVER THE ELEMENT OF SURPRISE

HONEY, HAVE YOU SEEN MY DENTURES?!
UH-OH
john Long
© 1990 by King Features Syndicate, Inc.
World rights reserved.

...AND THEN YOU HAD TO SAY... "SURE WE'LL BABY-SIT... NOOOOO PROBLEM"
Z Z Z Z
john Long
© 1990 by King Features Syndicate, Inc.
World rights reserved.
BURGER BUNDLES

john long

FLEM AND BARB WEARING THE NEW MR. AND MRS. POTATO HEAD SUNGLASSES

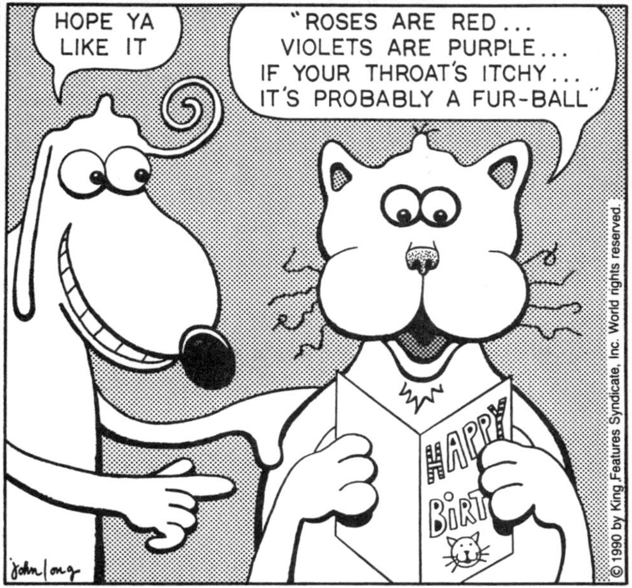

HOPE YA LIKE IT
"ROSES ARE RED... VIOLETS ARE PURPLE... IF YOUR THROAT'S ITCHY... IT'S PROBABLY A FUR-BALL"
HAPPY
BIRT
john long

WINSTON MADE A BIRTHDAY CARD FOR KIK.

WHY DON'T THEY DO SOMETHING ?
STILL NO SIGN OF INTELLIGENT LIFE ON THIS PLANET
STREET NEWS
© 1990 by King Features Syndicate, Inc.
World rights reserved.
john long

LET'S GO TO THE HOP...
OH BABY
john long
© World rights reserved.
1990 by King Features Syndicate

THE ROOS BROTHERS...GET DOWN...UP...DOWN...

Afterword

You have just been a part of an out-of-body experience in another dimension called the LONG OVERDUE zone. If you had missed the previous trip, you may now find yourself experiencing flashbacks of slap-happy watermelons, overeducated chameleons, or even of that little scamp Winston, the smart-aleck dog who never met a fire hydrant he didn't like. Under extreme circumstances, however, you may find yourself attempting strange things with kitchen utensils, like the all-new-all-you-can-eat-through-a-colander diet. Or the avid gardener and pizza lover may take a crack at the all-you-can-suck-through-a-fifty-foot-garden-hose diet. In all cases, we regret that we cannot be held responsible for any misuse of the contents of this book.

You are probably wondering how the Geeky Brothers turned up on the cover of this book, frolicking in the front yard, and in only their birthday suits, no less. At first we thought, "Jeez . . . wouldn't it be great to have some well-known folks say a few kind and clever words about this book." After all, it seems to work with "Entertainment Tonight," so we figured it would work here. We pulled together a list of our all-time favorite media gurus and fired out a note requesting the honor of their participation. The first went to Woody Allen, then Dave Letterman, followed by Bart Simpson, Basil Rathbone, and Spike Lee. It seems everyone has a different view of LONG OVERDUE, judging from the responses we received. As a matter of fact, we, too, found ourselves scratching our heads in amazement. With the drone of "We need a celebrity endorsement" pounding in his head, John came up with kind of a neat idea to get a picture of an Elvis impersonator for the cover. "Nothing like a nude imitation Elvis to bag their eyeballs on the bookshelf," John said. But without all the Spandex, that poor guy just didn't have a chance.

Turns out, he looked more like a chicken without the feathers. Another mild deterrent was that the head man at S&S wasn't too hot for the idea of a naked Elvis impersonator for the cover. "Great way to get your thigh tops (see page 69) kicked out of every B. Dalton in the country," he moaned. Anyway, we thought it was a pretty cool idea . . . but maybe it was just a little too weird even for us. With the hot breath of the deadline blowing down our shirt collar, the big guy anxiously suggested John "just draw something." At that point John had to get clever and luckily the Geeky Brother were available, and the rest is history. Thank God for those lawn ornaments.

With naked MOOS BROS. on the first cover, and naked GEEKY BROTHERS on the second cover, no doubt you are wondering what will show up on the cover of the next book. Will it be a latex Liz Taylor performing the dance of a thousand veils? Or . . . maybe some cheesy snapshots of the Nude Festival in Osaka? You probably ask, "At this rate, will I need to show I.D. to buy the next book?"

Well, as you know, cartoonists and authors in general are recognized for their high standards of good taste and fair play. For example, would a successful guy like Don Trump simply "trump up" a huge media event by dumping his wife for some little chick-a-daro, then flush the rest of his empire down the tubes . . . just in order to be #1 on the "Best Seller" list?

. . . On second thought . . . just in case . . . better bring I.D. next time.

Legal Notice—The foregoing has been the product of an alien's imagination. Any resemblance to actual events, locales or persons is entirely an honest mistake.